Three...Two...One...Blastoff!

MOLLY MAC

by MARTY KELLEY

PICTURE WINDOW BOOKS
a capstone imprint

This book is dedicated to Duncan, Meredith, Jana, and all the other amazing people at The Children's Literacy Foundation.–Marty

Molly Mac is published by
Picture Window Books
A Capstone Imprint
1710 Roe Crest Drive
North Mankato, MN 56003
www.mycapstone.com

Text © 2018 Marty Kelley
Illustrations © 2018 Marty Kelley

Education Consultant: Julie Lemire
Editor: Shelly Lyons
Designer: Ashlee Suker

Library of Congress Cataloging-in-Publication Data
Names: Kelley, Marty, author, illustrator.
Title: Three . . . two . . . one . . . blastoff! / by Marty Kelley. Description: North Mankato, Minnesota: Picture Window Books, [2018] Series: Molly Mac Summary: Molly's class is going on a field trip to the Space Science Center, and, despite what everyone tells her, Molly is convinced that they will find a real rocket there and blast off into outer space–but when she sneaks away from the class and tries to take off in the "spaceship" she finds herself totally grounded.

Identifiers: LCCN 2017040864 (print)
LCCN 2017044701 (ebook)
ISBN 9781515823872 (hardcover)
ISBN 9781515823957 (eBook PDF)

Subjects: LCSH: School field trips–Juvenile fiction. Science museums–Juvenile fiction. Space vehicles–Models–Juvenile fiction. Elementary schools–Juvenile fiction. CYAC: School field trips–Fiction. Science museums–Fiction. Museums–Fiction. Space vehicles–Fiction. Schools–Fiction. Classification: LCC PZ7.K28172 (ebook) LCC PZ7.K28172 Th 2018 (print) DDC [E]–dc23 LC record available at https://lccn.loc.gov/2017040864

Printed in the United States of America.
010835S18

★ Table of Contents ★

All About Me!

A picture of me!

Name:
Molly Mac

People in my family:
Mom
Dad
Drooly baby brother Alex

My best friend: KAYLEY!!!!

I really like:
Crunchy delicious tacos!
But not if they have tomatoes on them.
Yuck! They are squirty and wet.

When I grow up I want to be:
An artist. And a famous animal trainer.
And a professional taco taster. And a teacher.
And a super hero. And a lunch lady. And a pirate!

My special memory: Kayley and I camped in my
yard. We made s'mores with cheese. They
were surprisingly un-delicious.

Chapter 1

Space Toast!

Shhhk. Tick, tick, tick . . . ding!

Molly put two pieces of toast into a bag.

She put the bag into the freezer.

"Molly Mac?" Mom asked.

"Don't ask," Molly answered.

"I'm asking," said Mom.

"Well, we were talking about outer space

in school yesterday," Molly said.

"Yes, you told me about that," Mom said.

She strapped Alex into his high chair. She got

out his favorite bowl and spoon.

"Mr. Rose said that astronauts eat

freeze-dried astronaut food," Molly explained.

"Mmm, hmmm," Mom agreed. She opened a jar of blueberry baby food and poured some into Alex's bowl. Alex gurgled and drooled.

"I'm going to have an astronaut breakfast today," Molly said. "I'm making freeze-dried toast. I put the toast in the freezer. Now I just have to figure out the drying part."

"Oh no, Molly," Mom said.

"Can I borrow your hair dryer?" Molly asked. "That might work."

"Molly — " Mom said again.

"Or can I use the clothes dryer?" asked Molly.

"Don't even think about it," Mom warned.

Dad zipped into the kitchen. "I'm late! I'm late!" he exclaimed. He opened the freezer to get an ice pack for his lunch. "Do I even want to know why there is a bag of toast in the freezer?" he asked.

"Probably not," Molly answered.

Chapter 2

The Field Trip Hat

Kayley and Molly sat at their school desks. "Why did you bring a bag of toast to school?" Kayley asked.

"Don't ask," Molly told her.

"I'm asking," said Kayley.

"My astronaut toast experiment didn't work," Molly told her. "Mom didn't want me to waste food, so I brought it here for a snack."

Mr. Rose walked to the front of the room with his hands behind his back. "Good morning, class! Can anyone guess what I have behind my back?"

"An automatic taco maker?" asked Molly.

"Two hundred-fifty chocolate donuts with rainbow sprinkles?" asked Rohan.

Mr. Rose shook his head.

"A pony?" asked Jillian.

"Two hundred-fifty chocolate donuts **without** rainbow sprinkles?" asked Rohan.

Mr. Rose shook his head. "No, no, no. It's even better than any of those things."

He pulled his hands from behind his back. Then he held up an old, worn out baseball cap. A wide smile spread across his face.

"Excuse me, Mr. Rose?" Molly said. "You said it was better than any of those things. Your worn out, old hat is definitely not better than an automatic taco maker."

"Or a pony," said Jillian.

"Or two hundred-fifty chocolate donuts with rainbow sprinkles," sighed Rohan.

"This isn't any ordinary hat," Mr. Rose explained.

"Can it make tacos?" Molly asked.

"Is there a pony inside it?" asked Jillian.

"Is it almost snack time?" asked Rohan.

"This is my field trip hat!" Mr. Rose announced. "On Friday we are going on a field trip to the Space Science Center!"

The class cheered.

Molly's eyes lit up. She pointed to her bag of toast and smiled at Kayley. "Now I can learn how to make freeze-dried space toast from a **REAL** astronaut!"

Chapter 3

No Time for Applesauce

RIIIIIINNNNNGGG!!

The recess bell rang. Molly and Kayley raced across the playground to their secret snack spot.

Kayley opened her lunch box. She took out a container of applesauce and a spoon.

Molly held up her bag of cold, crumbled toast. "Can I perhaps interest you in a snack trade?" Molly asked.

Kayley poked the bag with her spoon. "I don't think so, Molly," she replied.

"Do you think Lunch Lady Deb could use her lunch-lady superpowers to turn this into delicious French toast?" Molly asked.

"Probably not," Kayley said. "I'll share my applesauce with you, though."

Molly shook her head. "No thanks," she said. "I've got a lot of planning to do. I don't have time for applesauce."

Molly pulled her sketchbook and a pencil out of her backpack.

"What are you planning for?" Kayley asked.

"The field trip to the Space Science Center!" Molly said. "I've never been to space before. I want to make sure I don't forget anything."

"Ummmm . . . Molly?" Kayley said. "I don't think we're going to space."

Molly rolled her eyes. "Of course we're going to space," she said. "Mr. Rose said we're going on a field trip to the Space Science Center, right? It has *space* right in the name. It **HAS** to be in space. That's the law. You can't call it the Space Science Center if it's not in space."

"Are you sure, Molly?" Kayley asked.

"Yup," Molly said. "It's like Silly Squirrel. He has the word *silly* right in his name. And what is he like?"

"He's silly," said Kayley.

"See? It's the law," Molly said.

"**Wow**," Kayley said. "This is going to be a great field trip. Going to space might even be more amazing than the time we went on a class trip to the post office!"

"And there won't be an angry post office lady there to yell at me about the stamp problem we had," Molly said. "How was I supposed to know that you can't actually use them to mail yourself to Hawaii?"

Kayley nodded. "Yeah. Going to space will definitely be better than peeling stamps off your face."

"I know!" Molly said. Plus, I'll get to ask a real astronaut how to make space toast!"

Molly tapped her pencil on the blank page of her sketchbook. "So how many pieces of toast do you think we should pack for the trip?" she asked.

Chapter 4

Space Bears and Laser Blasters

That afternoon, Molly Mac raced through the door of her house. She was waving a piece of paper over her head. "Mom! Mom! Mom! We need to go shopping!" she yelled. "I need one hundred pieces of toast and a laser blaster!"

Baby Alex squealed when he saw Molly.

Molly ran over and patted Alex on the head. "Hi, baby buddy! I'm going to miss you when I'm in space."

Mom closed the book she was reading to Alex. She reached over and gave Molly a hug. "Do I even want to know what you're talking about, Molly?"

"We probably both know the answer to that already, don't we?" Molly answered.

Mom laughed and nodded her head. "Yes, but why don't you tell me anyway?" she asked.

Molly held up her list. "Our class is going on a field trip to the Space Science Center on Friday!" she told Mom. "I'm going to meet real astronauts. They can teach me how to make real freeze-dried space toast!"

Mom took the list and read it.

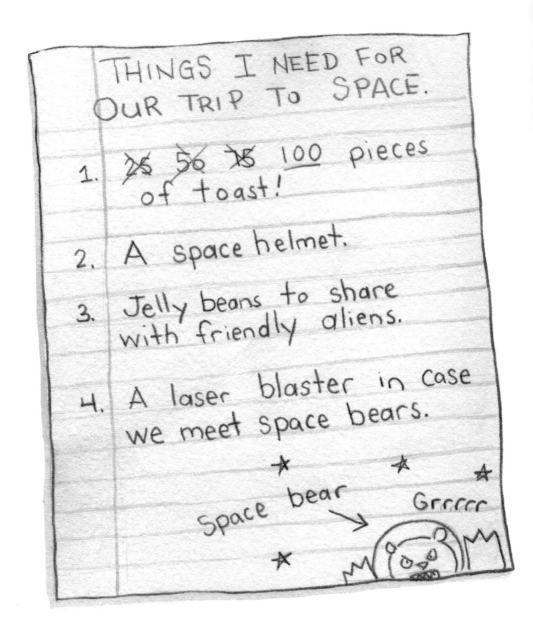

"Space bear?" Mom asked. She handed the list back to Molly.

"Don't ask," Molly said. She pointed to her list. "Mr. Rose told us that there is a group of stars named after a big bear. I don't want to meet a space bear. And I'm not sure where the laser blasters are at the store. Maybe next to the batteries?"

"Molly," Mom said. "I think we need to talk about this field trip."

"Me, too!" she said. "Do you think we can get more cinnamon raisin bread? This is a special occasion!"

"Molly," Mom laughed. "Kids don't go to outer space for a field trip."

Molly shook her head and sighed. She put her arm around her mother. "I know things have changed since you went to school ten million years ago," Molly said. "Nowadays, it's like the future at school. We have laptop computers and a whiteboard with electronic markers. We have an electric pencil sharpener named Mr. Munchy. We even have a magic box on the wall that sounds just like the principal when it talks. It's not like the olden days when you went to school."

"I'm sure it's not," Mom agreed. "But you are not going to space, Molly."

Molly laughed. "Nice try, Mom, but you can't trick me," she said. "Mr. Rose even has a special field trip hat. It will keep his hair looking nice when we are floating around in space."

Molly hopped off the chair and grabbed her backpack. She held it up. "Do you think I will be able to fit one hundred pieces of cinnamon raisin toast in here?"

Chapter 5

New Plan

The next day at school, Molly Mac plopped down in her seat. She leaned over to Kayley and asked, "Do you think your mom could take us shopping?"

Kayley scratched her head. "What do you need to go shopping for?" she asked.

Molly pulled her list out of her pocket. She spread it out on her desk. "I need to get one hundred pieces of cinnamon raisin toast. And a space helmet. And a laser blaster."

Kayley opened her mouth to ask a question. Molly interrupted her. "Space bears," she said. "Don't ask."

"I'm asking," Kayley said.

"I'm trying to pack for the field trip to space on Friday, but my parents are not cooperating," Molly said. "My mom told me our class is not going to space."

"My parents said the same thing!" Kayley told her.

"I explained the law to her," Molly said. "But I don't think she understood. She's 31 years old. She gets confused sometimes. She doesn't understand this modern world we live in."

Kayley shook her head. "I know what you mean," she said.

"I think I need to talk to Mr. Rose about this," Molly said. She grabbed her list and hopped out of her seat. She walked up to Mr. Rose's desk and knocked on it.

Mr. Rose took a long sip of coffee and placed his mug on the desk. "Good morning, Miss Mac. Why are you knocking on my desk?"

"You don't have a doorbell," Molly said.

"I see," Mr. Rose answered. He took another long sip of coffee. "What can I do for you?"

Molly held up her list. "I'm a little worried about the field trip on Friday," she said.

Mr. Rose smiled. "There's nothing to worry about, Molly!" he replied. "I have my field trip hat!" He pulled the hat out of his top drawer and plopped it on his head.

Molly pointed to his hat. "Are you going to pull a taco out of there now?" she asked.

Mr. Rose showed Molly the inside of his hat. "Still no tacos. Or ponies. Or chocolate donuts with rainbow sprinkles," he said. "It's just a hat."

Molly sighed. "Can that hat protect us from the space bear?" she asked.

"Space bear?" Mr. Rose asked. He took off his hat and put it back in the drawer of his desk.

"My mom won't buy me a laser blaster for the field trip. I'm worried that we might meet a space bear when we're out in space," Molly explained.

"We're not going to space, Molly," Mr. Rose said. "We're going to the Space Science Center. It's in Milford."

Molly sighed. She patted Mr. Rose on the shoulder. "Nice try, Mr. Rose, but my mom already tried that joke on me. They can't call it the Space Science Center if it isn't in space. That's the law. Just like Silly Squirrel."

Mr. Rose took another big, long slurp of coffee. "It's called the Space Science Center because we go there to **learn** about space. And science."

Molly's shoulders slumped. "So we're really not going into space?"

Mr. Rose shook his head.

"And there won't even be any astronauts there to teach me how to make space toast?" Molly asked.

"Sorry, kiddo," Mr. Rose said. "No astronauts. They do have a full-size model of a spaceship there, though. We get to walk through it and sit in the pilot's seat. It's so much fun. You'll love it!"

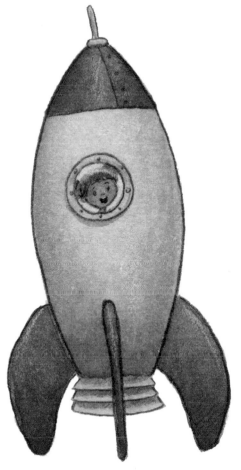

Molly's eyes grew wide. "We can sit in the pilot's seat of a real spaceship?" she asked.

Mr. Rose nodded. "Everybody gets a turn," he said.

A huge smile spread across Molly's face. She walked back to her desk and sat down.

"What did Mr. Rose say, Molly?" asked Kayley. "Are we going to space?"

"Oh yes, we are," Molly said. "Mr. Rose just doesn't know it yet."

Chapter 6

Field Trip Lunches

Friday morning, Molly Mac was sitting in her seat. Kayley skipped into class and heaved a bag onto her desk.

THUMP!!

"Wow!" Molly said. "What's in there?"

Kayley opened her bag. "It's the field trip lunch my dad packed for me," she said. "I have three peanut butter and jelly sandwiches, an apple, an orange, and a bag of cookies. There's a package of crackers and cheese and two chewy granola bars. And I have a water bottle, a bag of chips, some trail mix, a banana, another water bottle, and some after-dinner mints."

Kayley closed her bag and pointed to Molly's backpack. "What did you bring?" she asked.

Molly unzipped her backpack. She pulled out a small lunch box. "I have my lunch," she replied.

"That's it?" Kayley gasped. "We're going to be gone for four whole hours! Don't worry. I'll share my lunch with you so you don't starve to death. What else do you have in there?"

Molly bounced her eyebrows and smiled. "I have a drawing of my face that I glued to a Popsicle stick," she said.

"Do I even want to know why you made that, Molly?" asked Kayley.

"Probably not," Molly answered. "I also have safety goggles. I have my favorite fuzzy gloves. I have a bag of jelly beans to share with friendly aliens. I have some aluminum foil to make a helmet, in case I get sucked out into space. And I have four pieces of cinnamon raisin toast so the astronauts can teach me how to make freeze-dried space toast."

"Ummm, Molly?" Kayley said. "Mr. Rose said that we aren't going to space and that we won't meet any astronauts."

Molly reached into her backpack and pulled out her sketchbook. "That's because Mr. Rose doesn't know The Secret Plan!" she replied.

Kayley's eyes grew wide. "What's The Secret Plan?" she asked.

Molly started to flip through her sketchbook, but Mr. Rose stood up at his desk and clapped his hands.

CLAP! CLAP! CLAP-CLAP-CLAP!

Mr. Rose held his hands up over his head and wiggled his fingers. "And now, ladies and gentlemen, the moment you have all been waiting for . . ."

Mr. Rose opened his top drawer and pulled out his field trip hat. **"TA-DAAAAH!"** he sang.

"Is there a pony in it **NOW**?" asked Jillian.

"Or chocolate donuts with rainbow sprinkles?" asked Rohan.

Mr. Rose held up the hat over his head and smiled. "No ponies. No donuts," he told them.

Molly shot her hand into the air.

"And no tacos, Molly!" Mr. Rose said. He put the hat on his head. "The bus is here. It's time to go to the Space Science Center. Please line up at the door!"

Molly shoved her sketchbook into her backpack. "I'll have to tell you about the plan later," she whispered to Kayley.

Chapter 7

Time for the Secret Plan

Once Molly and Kayley were in their bus seats, Kayley leaned over to Molly. "So what's The Secret Plan?" she asked.

Molly leaned over and whispered into Kayley's ear. "It's too risky to tell you The Secret Plan here. We'll have to wait until we get to the Space Science Center."

Soon, the bus stopped and the doors opened. A woman climbed on to the bus and talked with Mr. Rose for a minute.

Mr. Rose stood up. "Okay, class," he announced, "This is Miss Duncan. She's going to be guiding us through the Space Science Center today."

Miss Duncan smiled. "Before we go in to The Space Science Center, does anyone have any questions?" she asked.

"Are you an astronaut?" asked Ian.

"Are there ponies in space?" asked Jillian.

"When do we get a snack?" asked Rohan.

"Where is the gift shop?" asked Kerri. "I have five dollars!"

"Do they sell donuts at the gift shop?" asked Rohan.

"I have to go to the bathroom," said Ann.

"Me, too," said Tim.

"Me, too," said Katie.

"Me, too," whispered Mr. Rose.

Miss Duncan led the class into the Space Science Center. They joined a long line in front of the bathrooms.

"Whoa!" said Molly. "The Space Science Center doors open automatically! It's like being in the future! This place is amazing!"

"The doors at the grocery store do the same thing," Kayley said.

"Maybe we can go on a field trip to the grocery store next!" Molly said. "While we're there, we can . . ."

Molly stopped talking. Her eyes grew wide.

"We can what, Molly?" asked Kayley.

Molly didn't answer. She slowly raised her arms upward. "This is it," she whispered.

Kayley looked. "What?" she asked.

"This is the spaceship Mr. Rose told me about," Molly said. "It's right here next to us!" She put her backpack on the ground and unzipped it. "It's time for The Secret Plan."

Chapter 8

Space Toast, Here I Come!

Molly reached into her backpack. She pulled out the goggles and gloves. She slipped them on. She unfolded the foil and wrapped it around her head.

"What are you doing, Molly?" asked Kayley.

"I'm going to get on that spaceship and blast into space," Molly said. "I'm going to find an astronaut and learn how to make space toast!"

Kayley gasped. "You can't leave the group!" she pleaded. "Mr. Rose said we all have to stick together!"

"The spaceship is right here," Molly said. She patted the side of the ship. "This line for the bathroom has about . . ." Molly quickly counted. "Eleventy hundred ba-jillion people in it. I'm going to get in the spaceship and blast off. I'll learn how to make space toast and get back here before Mr. Rose even knows I'm gone."

"But what if he comes over here?" Kayley asked.

Molly smiled and reached back into her bag. She took out the drawing of her face on the stick. She handed it to Kayley. "Then you hold this up. He'll never know the difference. It looks exactly like me."

Kayley grabbed the stick and looked at the picture of Molly. "This is a really bad idea, Molly," Kayley said.

"This is the best idea ever," Molly said. She grabbed her bag of toast and ducked through the door of the spaceship.

As soon as Molly went through the door, Mr. Rose walked over to Kayley. "After we all use the bathrooms we will be . . ." Mr. Rose scratched his head. "Where is Molly Mac?" he asked.

Kayley's eyes grew wide. She held up the paper face that Molly had given her. "Here I am, Mr. Rose," she said out of the corner of her mouth. "Yup. It's me. Molly Mac. It's really me. Definitely not just a face glued to a Popsicle stick."

Mr. Rose frowned and lifted the paper face out of Kayley's hand.

"Where did Molly go?" he asked.

Kayley pointed to the door of the spaceship.

Inside the ship, Molly looked around at all the flashing lights and screens. She saw the pilot's seat. It was empty! She ran over and sat down. The control stick was right in front of her. She grabbed it tightly. Then she held her finger over a flashing green button. **"Three ... two ... one ... space toast, here I come!"** she exclaimed.

Molly pushed the glowing green button and held on to the control stick.

Nothing happened.

She pushed the button again.

And again.

And again.

Molly looked at the screens and lights in the control panel. "Is this thing out of gas?" she asked. "Come on, spaceship. I have to learn how to make space toast and get back here before it's time for lunch!"

Molly was about to push the green button one more time when a hand landed on her shoulder. She spun around to see Mr. Rose standing behind her. He did not look happy.

"**Molly Mac!** You are in big trouble, young lady."

Chapter 9

Best Field Trip Ever, Worst Field Trip Ever

Molly sat slumped in her seat on the bus ride home. Kayley wrapped her arm around Molly. "That was the best field trip ever!" she said. "Except for the part when you got in trouble and had to hold Mr. Rose's hand for the rest of the day."

Molly frowned. "That was the worst field trip ever," she replied. "I didn't get to blast off into space. I didn't get to meet any astronauts. I didn't learn how to make freeze-dried space toast. I didn't even get to go into the gift shop. Mr. Rose made me spend all my time looking at moon rocks. And his hand was sweaty."

"You didn't get eaten by a space bear, though," Kayley said. "That's good."

Molly shrugged. "I guess," she sighed.

"And," Kayley said, "I got you something at the gift shop!"

Kayley reached into her backpack and pulled out two small foil packages. She handed one to Molly.

Molly took it and read the words printed on the front.

Chapter 10

Plan B

Molly gasped. **"Wow! Space Ice Cream!"** she exclaimed. "That's **WAY** better than space toast. Thanks, Kayley!"

"I bought a few extras because I was still hungry after lunch," Kayley said. She pointed to two more foil packages in her bag. "Let's try it!"

They tore open the packages and pulled out small, brown, white, and pink squares.

"**Wow!**" they gasped.

"Real Space Ice Cream," Molly said.

"Let's try it together," Kayley said.

They slowly raised the ice cream to their mouths. They both took a bite at the same time.

They chewed slowly for a minute.

"**Blaughck!**" coughed Molly.

"**Uggghhh!**" moaned Kayley.

They both spit out the ice cream.

"That's disgusting!" said Kayley.

Molly wiped her tongue with her sleeve. "That's nasty!" she cried.

Molly pulled the bag of cinnamon raisin toast from her backpack. "If space ice cream tastes that bad, can you imagine how horrible space toast must be?" she asked. "I'm glad I didn't learn how to make it. Now I can try Plan B with this toast."

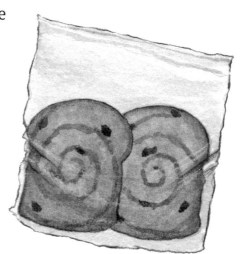

"Do I even want to know what Plan B is, Molly?" asked Kayley.

"Probably not," Molly said.

All About Me!

A picture of me!

Name:

Marty Kelley

People in my family:

My lovely wife, Kerri

My amazing son, Alex

My terrific daughter, Tori

I really like: Pizza! And hiking in the woods. And being with my friends. And reading. And making music. And traveling with my family.

When I grow up I want to be:

A rock star drummer!

My special memory: Sitting on the couch with my kids and reading a huge pile of books together.

Find more at my website: www.martykelley.com

GLOSSARY

astronaut (AS-truh-nawt)—a person who is trained to live and work in space

automatic (aw-tuh-MAT-ik)—able to operate without help from a person

cooperate (koh-OP-uh-rayt)—to work with others and to follow rules

experiment (ik-SPEER-uh-muhnt)—a scientific test to find out how something works

freeze-dry (FREEZ-drye)—to dry in a vacuum while frozen in order to preserve

laser (LAY-zur)—a thin, intense, high-energy beam of light

modern (MOD-urn)—up-to-date or new in style

occasion (uh-KAY-zhuhn)—a special or important event

pilot (PYE-luht)—a person who flies an aircraft

TALK ABOUT IT

1. Why does Molly want to make freeze-dried toast? What is real astronaut food like?

2. What might Molly be referring to when she says "space bears?"

3. Did Molly make a good decision when she sneaked into the spaceship? What could she have done differently?

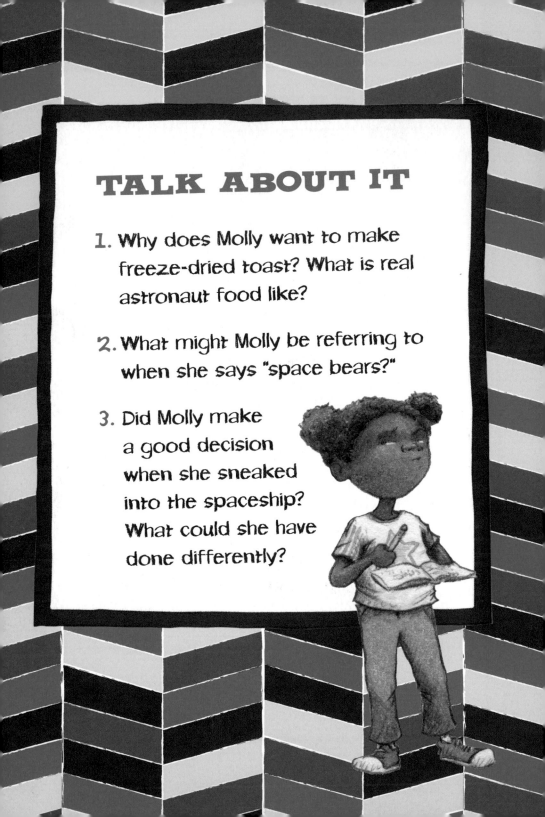

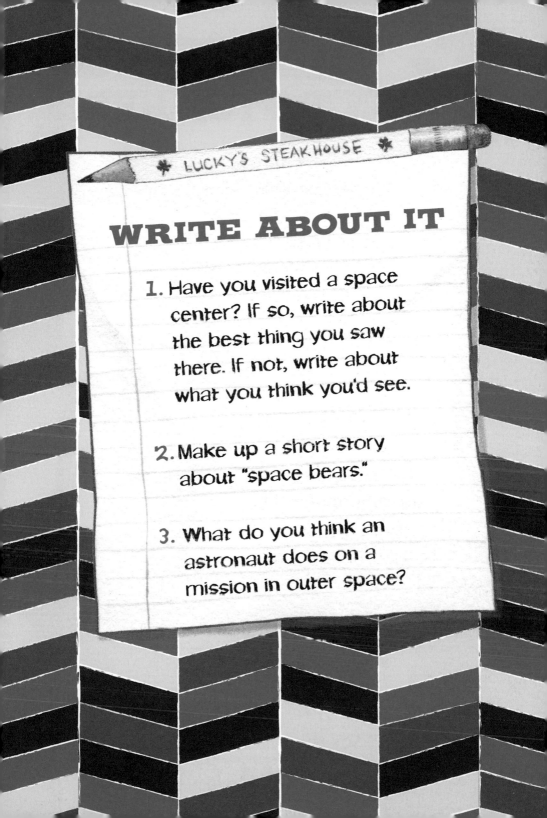

WRITE ABOUT IT

LUCKY'S STEAKHOUSE ✳

1. Have you visited a space center? If so, write about the best thing you saw there. If not, write about what you think you'd see.

2. Make up a short story about "space bears."

3. What do you think an astronaut does on a mission in outer space?

THE FUN
DOESN'T STOP HERE!

Discover more at
www.capstonekids.com

★ Videos & Contests

★ Games & Puzzles

★ Friends & Favorites

★ Authors & Illustrators

Find cool websites and more books like this one
at **www.facthound.com**.

Just type in the Book ID: **9781515823872**
and you're ready to go!

Lucky Break

Tooth Fairy Trouble

Top Secret Author Visit

MOLLY MAC
by MARTY KELLEY

MOLLY MAC
by MARTY KELLEY